Finn and the Magic Goat

For Fynn, Oscar, Sage, Olivia and Frances – MG

First published in 2008
by Wayland

This paperback edition published in 2009

Wayland
338 Euston Road
London NW1 3BH

Wayland Australia
Level 17/207 Kent Street
Sydney, NSW 2000

Series Editor: Louise John
Editor: Katie Powell
Cover design: Paul Cherrill
Design: D.R.ink
Consultant: Shirley Bickler

A CIP catalogue record for this book is available from the British Library.

ISBN 9780750254687 (hbk)
ISBN 9780750254694 (pbk)

Printed in China

Wayland is a division of Hachette Children's Books,
an Hachette Livre UK company

www.hachettelivre.co.uk

Finn and the Magic Goat

Written by Mick Gowar
Illustrated by Tim Archbold

WAYLAND

It was the first day of the Sligo
Fair and Finn was trying to sell
his two goats.

He sold young Billy for two golden
sovereigns, but no one wanted to buy
old Nanny.

"I'm sure I'll sell her in the morning,"
thought Finn.

As Finn was settling down to sleep, two men came to the goat pen. They didn't see Finn lying in the hay.

"Did you see that fool with the goat?"
asked the skinny man.
"I did," said his chubby friend.

"I saw him sell his billy goat this morning. He's got two gold sovereigns. When he comes back tomorrow we'll snatch his purse and run away!"

They both laughed nasty laughs.

"What am I going to do?" muttered Finn. "Those thieving rogues are going to try and steal my money."

"Maybe I can help?" said a voice
behind him.

"Who said that?" asked Finn, looking
behind him in alarm.

"I did," said the goat. "I don't want to be sold to a stranger. If I help you, will you keep me?"

"I certainly will," said Finn.

"Here's my plan," said the goat. "You hide one gold sovereign in each of my ears. When those bad men come back tomorrow, this is what you must do..."

The next morning, the two evil fellows crept up to the goat pen.

"They're back," whispered Nanny.
"Quick, now! Do as I told you."

"Dear Nanny, give me some money!"
cried Finn in a loud voice, and he pulled
her beard.

Nanny shook her head and a gold
sovereign shot out of her ear into
Finn's hand.

Finn pulled Nanny's beard again and cried, "Dear Nanny, give me some money." A gold sovereign fell out of her other ear.

"It's a magic goat," gasped the fat thief. "We must buy it!" said the skinny thief.

At the fair that day, the fat man
said to Finn, "We'll give you twenty
sovereigns for your goat. What do
you say?"

"Agreed," said Finn.

"We're going to be rich," whispered the fat man.

"I know," the thin man replied.

The fat thief knelt down in front of
Nanny. He pulled her beard and said,
"Dear Nanny, give me some money."

But nothing happened.

"Try pulling her beard a little harder,"
suggested the thin one.

So the fat thief pulled Nanny's beard harder. "Dear Nanny, give me some money," he said.

"Still not hard enough," said the thin man.

So the fat thief pulled Nanny's beard with all his might. Nanny put her head down and butted him as hard as she could in the stomach.

Nanny jumped over the pen and galloped down the road.

"Waaagh!" yelled the fat man. "Stop her! She's getting away!"

Nanny leapt onto the back of Jim's cart just as it was driving out of the town gates.

"Well done, Nanny!" said Finn. "We've got twenty sovereigns. We're rich!"

"I don't think so," said Jim. He pointed to the note. "It says 'Bank of Toyland' where it should say 'Bank of Ireland.' That money's fake!"

And he laughed all the way home.

START READING is a series of highly enjoyable books for beginner readers. **The books have been carefully graded to match the Book Bands widely used in schools.** This enables readers to be sure they choose books that match their own reading ability.

Look out for the Band colour on the book in our Start Reading logo.

The Bands are:

Pink Band 1

Red Band 2

Yellow Band 3

Blue Band 4

Green Band 5

Orange Band 6

Turquoise Band 7

Purple Band 8

Gold Band 9

START READING books can be read independently or shared with an adult. They promote the enjoyment of reading through satisfying stories supported by fun illustrations.

Mick Gowar has written more than 70 books for children, and likes to visit schools and libraries to give readings and lead workshops. He has also written plays and songs, and has worked with many orchestras. Mick writes his books in a shed in Cambridge.

Tim Archbold believes that making your fortune can be a difficult thing to do. Grumpy kings are hard to please, magic goats are always difficult to work with and the end of a rainbow is just over the next hill. But keep trying and have some fun on the way to your fortune...